Elephant's Trunk

God made the wild animals according to their kind, the livestock according to their kinds, and all creatures that move along the ground according to their kinds. And God saw that it was good. GENESIS 1:25

And God saw everything that he had made, and behold, it was very good. GENESIS 1:31A

Elephant's Trunk

First Edition

Copyright © 2001 by Scheer Delight Publishing, P.O. Box 21224, Wichita, Kansas 67208-1224. All rights reserved. No part of this publication may be reproduced, stored in a retrieval system, or transmitted in any form or by any means, electronic, mechanical, photocopying, recording, or otherwise, without the prior permission of the copyright holder.

Library of Congress Control Number 2001118637

ISBN 0-9671761-2-3

Printed in the U.S.A. by Mennonite Press, Inc., Newton, Kansas 67114

Scheer Delight Publishing
...on the cutting edge

Ruth Scheer

Illustrated by Faye Grable

Elephant's Trunk

lephant's trunk is the handiest thing,

The longest of noses any animal can bring!

For smelling and breathing and taking in air;

Flexible, movable—all with great flair!

lephant's trunk has two tusks just outside,

Long-growing teeth made of ivory inside;

Useful for rooting a dry water hole,

Or carrying logs, large loads or a pole.

lephant's trunk can pick up a tree,

Place it wherever she wants it to be;

Handy for carrying—muscular, strong!

Can you imagine a nose that's so long?

Elephant's trunk rises high in the air;

Trumpeting wildly, she announces she's there!

A true pachyderm, a humongous beast;

Inch-thick gray skin, wrinkled and creased.

lephant's trunk grows from hole in her head;

"Africa-shaped" ears, either side, <u>huge</u> are spread;

Flapping of ears cools the blood flowing through,

Air-conditioning several tons of sinew!

 lephant's trunk flexes right above feet;

Toes rest on pads; she can run fast and fleet!

At end of short tail are just a few hairs,

A perfect fly swatter for any pest who dares!

lephant's trunk writhes and wallows in mud,

Spreading the "armor" with soft-sounding thud;

Keeping off insects that bite and that sting

All of the elephants and their offspring.

lephant's trunk is a snorkel supreme,

For swimming so gracefully under a stream;

Then at shore's edge, the trunk gives a shower,

A-spraying herself with water and power!

lephant's trunk reaches up into trees,

For succulent greenery, stems and high leaves;

Much like giraffe with his long stretching neck,

While short ones give up and say,

"Oh! What the heck!"

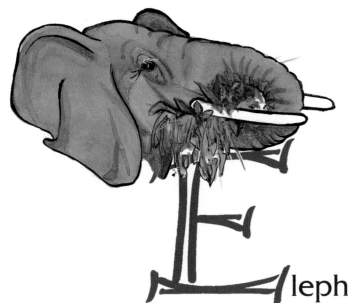

lephant's trunk grabs up sweet smelling hay,

Puts it in mouth—stuffs it back all the way!

Chewing and grinding with molars for teeth,

Ever replaced when they've worn down beneath.

lephant's trunk has two fingers that bend

Placed at the uttermost farthest tip end;

Scouring the ground with precision and deft,

Retrieving each delicate morsel that's left!

lephant's trunk is all ready to go—

Anywhere, anytime—how <u>convenient</u> to grow

Attached to her head between her two eyes,

A most helpful schnoz for her leviathan size!

Elephant's trunk is the handiest thing,
The longest of noses any animal can bring!
> For smelling and breathing and taking in air;
> Flexible, movable—all with great flair!

Elephant's trunk has two tusks just outside,
Long-growing teeth made of ivory inside;
> Useful for rooting a dry water hole,
> Or carrying logs, large loads or a pole.

Elephant's trunk can pick up a tree,
Place it wherever she wants it to be;
> Handy for carrying—muscular, strong!
> Can you imagine a nose that's so long?

Elephant's trunk rises high in the air;
Trumpeting wildly, she announces she's there!
> A true pachyderm, a humongous beast;
> Inch-thick gray skin, wrinkled and creased.

Elephant's trunk grows from hole in her head;
"Africa-shaped" ears, either side, huge are spread;
> Flapping of ears cools the blood flowing through,
> Air-conditioning several tons of sinew!

Elephant's trunk flexes right above feet;
Toes rest on pads; she can run fast and fleet!
> At end of short tail are just a few hairs,
> A perfect fly swatter for any pest who dares!

Elephant's trunk writhes and wallows in mud,
Spreading the "armor" with soft-sounding thud;
> Keeping off insects that bite and that sting
> All of the elephants and their offspring.

Elephant's trunk is a snorkel supreme,
For swimming so gracefully under a stream;
> Then at shore's edge, the trunk gives a shower,
> A-spraying herself with water and power!

Elephant's trunk reaches up into trees,
For succulent greenery, stems and high leaves;
> Much like giraffe with his long stretching neck,
> While short ones give up and say, "Oh! What the heck!"

Elephant's trunk grabs up sweet smelling hay,
Puts it in mouth—stuffs it back all the way!
> Chewing and grinding with molars for teeth,
> Ever replaced when they've worn down beneath.

Elephant's trunk has two fingers that bend
Placed at the uttermost farthest tip end;
> Scouring the ground with precision and deft,
> Retrieving each delicate morsel that's left!

Elephant's trunk is all ready to go—
Anywhere, anytime—how convenient to grow
> Attached to her head between her two eyes,
> A most helpful schnoz for her leviathan size!

Vocabulary Words

flexible (flĕk′sɛ-bɛl) bends easily

flair (flâr) special ability

rooting (ro͞ot′ĭng) digging up

muscular (mŭs′kyɛ-lɛr) strong

trumpeting (trŭm′pĭt-ĭng) bellowing like a trumpet

pachyderm (păk′y-dêrm′) hooved animal with a thick skin

humongous (hyo͞o-mŏng′gɛs) very large

sinew (sĭn′yo͞o) tendons or fibrous cords giving strength

flexes (flĕks′ɛz) bends

writhes (rīthz) twists violently

wallows (wŏl′ōz) rolls about in mud

offspring (ôf′sprĭng) children

snorkel (snôr′kɛl) tube for breathing under water

succulent (sŭk′yɛ-lɛnt) juicy

molars (mō′lɛrz) teeth for grinding

uttermost (ŭt′ɛr-mōst′) extreme

scouring (skour′ĭng) completely searching an area

precision (prĭ-sĭzh′ɛn) accuracy

deft (dĕft) skill

retrieving (rĭ-trēv′ĭng) getting back

delicate (del′ĭ-kĭt) small and fine

morsel (môr′sɛl) a small piece, usually food

convenient (kɛn-vēn′yɛnt) handy

schnoz (shnŏz) nose

leviathan (lɛ-vī′ɛ-thɛn) whale-sized

Hippopotamus, My Friend

Hippopotamus is having spring fever! This exotic, bulky animal plays hide-n-seek. Holding her breath under water, then coming up to snort and look around, she repeats these antics over and over again. Watching her are two faithful friends—Feather the white water bird and Fin the orange fish. The friendship of these three such different creatures is whimsical yet factual.

Giraffe at the Zoo

A smart Giraffe thinks up a clever plan to reach the greener grass across the moat's ditch. He spreads his front legs in a widespread V and makes his neck a bridge to reach the grass. Looking on are the giraffe's three bird friends—the oxpecker tick bird, the vulture, and gold crowned crane. The charm of this story is the example of the giraffe's innovative self-reliance and belief in himself.

Elephant's Trunk

By example, a mother African elephant teaches her calf how to use its trunk in a variety of ways. Teaching the calf to accomplish the many activities such a verstile "nose" can perform is the mother elephant's maternal objective.

ORDER

Elephant's Trunk

and Grandmother Ruth's other books: **Hippopotamus, My Friend** and **Giraffe at the Zoo.**

Cost for each book is $9.95 (Kansans add $.59 sales tax per book). Add $3.00 shipping and handling for 1 to 9 books. FREE shipping for orders of 10 or more.

Write to:
Scheer Delight Publishing
P.O. Box 21224
Wichita, Kansas 67208-1224

Visit us on the web at
www.scheerdelightpub.com

"Grandmother Ruth" as Ruth Scheer is fondly called by her ten children and 29 grandchildren has led her family to "1973 Kansas Musical Family of the Year;" was 1987 Kansas Mother of the Year; and has served as president of the Alliance of the Kansas Dental Association, Wichita Alumni Chapter of Mu Phi Epsilon and Thursday Afternoon Music Club. One of her greatest joys is playing piano and accordion in family shows by the "Scheer Delights" with her husband, children and grandchildren.

Ruth graduated with honors from Wichita State University in 1948 with a major in English and minors in music and French. Her ambition is to become the "Grandma Moses" of classic children's literature, inspiring children to read that which is good and beautiful.

Faye Grable's enjoyment of color and drawing started at a very early age. She explored her gift of creativity at Wichita State University, Kansas City Art Institute, Kansas Newman University, and numerous artist led workshops. Faye is a member of The Art Guild of Wichita.

Faye's artistic talents have offered opportunities to explore various media. She has worked as a graphic artist and a teacher of fashion illustration and pastel. Expressions of her creativity include church fabric art, story illustration, and working as a team with her artist husband to create backdrops for melodramas and dinner theater. Faye and Jack have two children and four grandchildren.

Faye Grable and Ruth Scheer have been friends since college sorority days. They are sorority sisters in the local sorority Pi Kappa Psi. They are kindred spirits in their love for children and beauty. Both Ruth and Faye believe in the old-fashioned virtues of good taste and graciousness. Combining Ruth's musical poetry and Faye's expressive art bring to life the best in children's literature.